KEEKER

and the Springtime Surprise

by **HADLEY HIGGINSON** Illustrated by **LISA PERRETT**

chronicle books · san francisco

Chapter

1

This is Catherine Corey Keegan Dana, but everyone calls her Keeker. Keeker is ten. She lives in Vermont with her parents and a kazillion pets: five dogs, four cats, two hamsters, a goat, a goldfish, and a baby bird named Peep.

There's one big horse on Keeker's farm. And one very small (and sometimes sneaky) pony named Plum.

KEEKER

and the Springtime Surprise

Series design by Kristine Brogno and Mary Beth Fiorentino.
Book design by Mariana Oldenburg.
Typeset in Weiss Medium.
The illustrations in this book were rendered Adobe Illustrator.
Manufactured in China.

Barbie is a registered trademark of Mattel, Inc.

Library of Congress Cataloging-in-Publication Data
Higginson, Hadley.
Keeker and the springtime surprise / by Hadley Higginson;
illustrated by Lisa Perrett.
p. cm.
Summary: It is springtime in Vermont, and new life abounds along
with new baby groundhogs in Plum's field, and knowing how her
father feels about them, ten-year-old Keeker decides to stage a
"Save the Groundhogs" event.
ISBN-13 978-0-8118-5598-3 (library edition)
ISBN-10 0-8118-5598-8 (library edition)
ISBN-13 978-0-8118-5599-0 (pbk.)
ISBN-10 0-8118-5598-6 (pbk.)
[1. Farm life—Vermont—Fiction. 2. Animals—Infancy—Fiction.
3. Ponies—Fiction. 4. Theater—Fiction.]
I. Perrett, Lisa, ill. II. Title.
PZ7.53499Keek 2007
[E]—dc22
2006021106

Distributed in Canada by Raincoast Books
9050 Shaughnessy Street, Vancouver, British Columbia V6P 6E5

10 9 8 7 6 5 4 3 2 1

Chronicle Books LLC
680 Second Street, San Francisco, California 94107

www.chroniclekids.com

Springtime in Vermont can be quite surprising. When the snow finally melts, all sorts of things that have been hidden all year suddenly turn up.

The dogs find their old tennis balls. Keeker sometimes finds a lost Barbie doll or a toy tractor. And Plum often finds a halter that's been left on the ground by someone who was in a big hurry to go riding.

The other fun thing about spring is that there are baby animals just about everywhere. In fact, Keeker found Peep just sitting on the lawn, right next to her broken nest, peeping her head off.

Two of the dogs were sniffing around her, wondering what all the fuss was about.

"Oh, CUTE!" said Keeker, when she saw Peep. She picked her up very, very carefully and carried her inside.

Keeker's mom knew exactly what to do.

"That's a cedar waxwing," said Mrs. Dana. "They usually eat berries and bugs, so I think if we feed her some fruit and a little bit of meat, she'll be fine."

They made a home for Peep in Keeker's bathroom and fed her teeny tiny bits of raw hamburger and cut-up grapes.

The baby bird was as happy as she could be. She hopped around the bathroom, peeping at Keeker and pooping all over the place.

Keeker wasn't the only one with a new animal to take care of. A mama groundhog and six roly-poly groundhog babies had made a home in Plum's pasture.

This made Plum VERY nervous. She knew
that Keeker's dad didn't like groundhogs at all;
he always yelled and waved his arms at them.

(He wasn't trying to be mean; he just wanted to shoo them away. Groundhogs make holes in the ground that the horses can trip in.)

Plum didn't mind the holes, though. And she liked seeing Mrs. Groundhog and her pups waddling across the field.

But what to do about Mr. Dana?

"I wish they'd wait till after dark to strut around," thought Plum anxiously.

But Mrs. Groundhog was bold as brass. She paraded her babies in the bright light of day, not caring who saw them.

It was too worrisome. Plum needed to do something.

So every time the groundhogs went out, Plum went with them. She walked right next to

them, so that from the Danas' kitchen window, you couldn't see any pups.

"La dee da da," pretended Plum. "No groundhogs here!"

The groundhog babies didn't mind at all. They were cool and comfortable walking in Plum's shadow, and they liked it when her tail tickled their heads.

Of course, hiding something from Mr. Dana was one thing; hiding something from Keeker was quite another. Keeker noticed the groundhog babies right away.

"Oh, WOW!" she said when she saw them.

"Even Dad couldn't be mad at *these* groundhogs.
I'll get Mom to talk to him."

Keeker galloped off to find her mom.

Chapter

2

She looked all over the house—upstairs, downstairs, in the basement, and even in the garage. She looked in the vegetable garden and out in the shed. She checked down by the pond. Finally, Keeker just stood in the back-yard and hollered.

"MOOOOOOMMMM!" yelled Keeker.

"WHAAAAAAAT?" Mrs. Dana yelled back.

She was in the barn with Doc Thomas, the vet who took care of the animals at Keeker's house. Keeker's mom and Doc Thomas were standing outside of Pansy's stall, talking very seriously about something.

They didn't even notice when Keeker came up and didn't pay any attention when Keeker tugged on Mrs. Dana's sleeve or jiggled her elbow.

"MOOOOOOMMMM!" said Keeker.

"KEEKER!" said Mrs. Dana. "Honestly. What is it?"

"I want to SHOW you something," said Keeker. By this time, she was hopping back and forth from one foot to another because she just couldn't wait any longer. She knew her mom would love those fat baby groundhogs!

"Well, I'm sorry," said Mrs. Dana, "but I'm very busy right now. Pansy is due to have her foal any day now, and Doc and I need to make sure everything is ready."

Mrs. Dana's horse was going to have a baby (a foal is a baby horse), and that was all anyone talked about. Pansy, Pansy, Pansy. Keeker was sick of it! What about her? What about Plum?

Hmmmph. Keeker stopped hopping.

Since her mom was being no fun at all, Keeker went off to find her dad.

She found him outside his woodshop, standing in a big pile of lumber and looking frazzled. Goatie was rummaging around in the toolbox, seeing if there was anything in it that would be fun to eat.

"Dad!" said Keeker. "I have something really cool to show you. I know you THINK you

don't like groundhogs, but these are little baby
ones, and they're really cute and . . ."

"Not now, Keeker," said Mr. Dana, sounding
exasperated. I'm really busy. I need to work on
Pansy's stall, and I don't want to talk to you
about groundhogs. You know that they dig
holes! If you show them to me, I'm just going
to have to chase them away."

WHAT? Chase them away? They were so little—and so cute! Just thinking about it made Keeker want to cry.

Keeker lay down on the ground and worked up a gigantic tantrum.

"Oh, poor little baby groundhogs!" she sobbed, flailing her arms around.

Mr. Dana was not impressed. He just frowned and kept on hammering. Eventually, Keeker got tired of weeping and moaning, so she picked herself up and stomped off.

Keeker felt very cranky. Stupid Pansy and her stupid foal. It wasn't fair! Keeker went over to Plum's field and sat down under the apple tree, scratching her back against the bark the way Plum sometimes did.

"Nobody even CARES about us," said Keeker to Plum. "Everyone's all bothered about Pansy. I

bet we could run away, and no one would even notice."

Plum looked at Keeker suspiciously. Running away sounded like a lot of work. Plus, Plum had her groundhogs to take care of.

Keeker lay down in Plum's field and looked up. The clouds rolled and tumbled by, changing shape as they went. They looked like clowns. Or characters in a play.

A play. What an idea! A big, fancy play, with costumes and everything. That would impress her parents and give Keeker the perfect opportunity to ask for a favor. Keeker could see it now: her parents applauding and clapping, Keeker and Plum taking a bow, and then Keeker saying (rather grandly, of course), "This magnificent theatrical production was brought to you by the groundhogs. Save the groundhogs!"

A play would be just the ticket. It would help save the pups, and it would get everyone to forget about Pansy and the new foal, at least for a little while.

Chapter

3

Keeker was so excited she felt like she might explode. Instead, she ran over to Plum and hugged her hard around the neck.

"Won't this be cool?" said Keeker to Plum. "We can make costumes and everything."

"Gak!" snorted Plum. "Stop strangling me, you crazy girl."

But secretly, Plum thought it was brilliant.

Of course, the big question was: Which play should they do? Keeker thought of some stories she knew. "Cinderella." "Sleeping Beauty." "Snow White and the Seven Dwarfs." Blah. They all seemed babyish. Plus, there were no good pony parts.

Keeker decided to go dig in her parents'
library for inspiration. She ran back to the
house and got Peep and let her perch on her
shoulder. (Peep LOVED excursions to other
rooms.) They headed downstairs to the library.

The library was one of those rooms that
Keeker's mom liked to keep tidy, so usually

the door was shut (to keep the dogs out—and
quite possibly to keep Keeker out, too!).

Keeker always felt like she should be quiet
in the library, even though there was no one
in there to tell her to "shush." She tiptoed in
and started looking through the books on the
lowest shelves.

Most of them were big and heavy and had lots of pictures. Keeker started flipping through a world atlas, admiring all the cities and states and oceans and islands. Especially islands.

"Hmmm," murmured Keeker, "maybe we should do a play about pirates!"

Peep peeped at that. She was sure she would make an *excellent* pirate parrot!

But then again, it was very hard to fake an ocean. A land play would be better.

On the very top shelf, the books were very old—and very dusty. Most had cracked leather bindings and funny titles. Keeker climbed up on the back of the couch so she could see better.

At the end of the shelf was a BIG book, with its title in gold: *Don Quixote, Man of La Mancha.*

Don Kee-Ho-Tay. Keeker had heard of him! From what she remembered, he was kind of

like a knight, except that he fought windmills instead of dragons.

And, of course, he rode a horse. Perfect!

Keeker put Peep back in the bathroom and ran outside to find Plum. Plum was standing in the middle of the field—with her nose down a groundhog hole.

Plum hadn't seen the groundhog pups all day, and she was a little anxious.

"Where are they?" she wondered.

She sniffed and sniffed, but didn't smell any groundhog smells. All she smelled was dark dirt and grass roots. (And actually, it smelled quite delicious!) "I could stay here all day," sighed Plum.

Keeker left Plum to her sniffing (and groundhog spying), and went off to work on costumes.

Chapter

4

In the Don Quixote book, the clothes looked very old-timey. In fact, Don himself wore armor, like a medieval knight. But where in the world would Keeker find armor?

Just then, there was a loud CRASH. Keeker looked out the window and saw Goatie rooting around in the garbage cans. (Goatie LOVED garbage. He especially loved knocking

things over to get to it.) That gave Keeker a
fabulous idea.

Hmmm, maybe trash can lids would work?

Keeker went outside and found two lids. She
tied them together with some twine and hung
the whole thing over her head—and it looked
pretty great! It didn't look very royal, though.
And that Don Quixote guy thought a lot of
himself. . . .

"I need some feathers," thought Keeker. "Or something fancy. . . ."

Finding feathers turned out to be easy. There was a big pink feather duster in the kitchen closet. Keeker glued it onto her riding helmet. It looked MARVELOUS.

But what to do about Plum's costume?
Because, of course, she needed one, too.

In the book, the horses all wore big drapey
things under their saddles—things with tassels
and stuff along the bottom. Things that looked
an awful lot like . . . bedspreads!

Keeker trotted into her parents' bedroom
and grabbed the bedspread. It had a fringe and
everything. It was just right!

As for where the play would actually happen, well, that was obvious—Plum's field. In the book, Don Quixote liked to charge at windmills. Keeker and Plum could charge the apple tree.

Keeker dragged all the kitchen chairs down to the field, so her audience would have a place to sit. Then she hopped on Plum's back and went off to find her parents (to tell them all about the wonderful, amazing, spectacular play they were about to see).

Keeker and Plum clomped up onto the lawn, and Keeker yelled for her parents.

"MOOOMM! DAAAAADDD!"

No answer.

Plum took advantage of being up on the lawn by eating some daffodils. She loved it when Keeker rode her bareback. It was so much easier to get away with things.

After clomping all over the place for
almost an hour, Keeker and Plum finally found
Keeker's parents. They were in the barn again
(of course), all crowded around Pansy's stall

with Doc Thomas. GOSH. Couldn't they stop
thinking about Pansy, even for just one minute?

Plum hoped being pregnant wasn't something you could catch, like a cold. She gave a
little cough to see if she felt sick. (She didn't.)

"Mom! Dad!" said Keeker. "You HAVE to
come down to Plum's field in about an hour

because we have a big surprise for you. You'll come, right? You promise?"

"Ummm, sure," said Keeker's mom, looking at a chart Doc Thomas was holding.

"Of course, Keeker," said Keeker's dad, waving his hand kind of absentmindedly.

Keeker sighed. Parents could be so difficult.

Chapter 5

Keeker and Plum hurried back down to Plum's field and began to get ready. First, Keeker tied on the garbage can lids, to make her clanky armor, and put on her feathered riding hat.

Then she used a marker to draw a very grand and curly mustache on herself. Voilá!

Plum's costume was easy. All Keeker had to do was drape the bedspread over Plum's back.

It didn't seem quite right, though. Something was missing . . . so Keeker drew a mustache on Plum, too.

Everything was ready. It was time to put on the play and save the groundhogs! Keeker decided to hide the groundhogs in the hollow part of Plum's apple tree. Then at the end of the play (when everyone was wildly clapping and cheering), she would come out and say, "This play is dedicated to our WONDERFUL groundhog family."

Then the groundhogs would waddle out, and her parents would fall in love with them, and everything would be fine. It was a fool-proof plan.

Plum stuck her nose down one of the groundhog holes and snorted as loud as she could. She did that a few more times, and eventually Mrs. Groundhog and all her babies came hurrying out of the other hole, looking grumpy.

Plum used her nose to very gently herd them over to the apple tree.

Keeker looked at her watch—it was almost showtime! She and Plum practiced charging a few times (Keeker used a broom instead of a lance) and then went behind the apple tree to wait for their audience.

They waited. And waited, and waited, and waited. Where WERE they? The groundhogs had all fallen asleep in a big furry pile. (It was very dark and cozy inside the apple tree.) And

even Plum was getting a little snoozy. (It was
very comfortable under the bedspread.)

"Sheesh," said Keeker. "This is getting ridicu-
lous. Come on, Plum."

Keeker stuck her lance (er, broomstick) in the air and gave Plum a mighty kick. Plum reared up a bit, making the bedspread flap impressively.

And they charged up to the barn. The groundhogs woke up with a start, came tumbling out of the apple tree, and waddled right after them!

"Ta-da ta-dum! Behold Don Quixote!" yelled Keeker, as they clattered (and flapped and

clanked) into the barn. But it was so, so quiet in there that she immediately felt weird. It was like the "shush" feeling in the library!

Keeker's parents and Doc Thomas were all in Pansy's stall. Keeker and Plum tiptoed down there and peeked over the edge of the door. Mrs. Groundhog and all the pups tiptoed down, too, and snuck *under* the stall door (where there was a nice big crack—just right for sneaking).

Pansy was standing quietly in the corner. All the grown-ups were clustered around her. And standing right in the middle was . . . the cutest, spindliest, sweetest-looking brand-new baby horse, still covered in goo and looking very wobbly on her legs.

"Ohhhhh," said Keeker.

"Wowie," thought Plum.

"Squeak!" squeaked the groundhogs. They were very impressed.

"Hey, you two," said Keeker's mom happily. "Say hello to Rosie—Pansy's very first foal!"

"Isn't she a beauty?" said Mr. Dana. He sounded a little choked up. Plum realized this was the perfect time to introduce the *other* babies. She stamped her foot a little, and Mr. Dana looked down and saw all six groundhog pups piled up and looked as sweet as can be.

Mrs. Groundhog felt very proud. Her babies were so well behaved!

Mr. Dana bent down with a big smile on his face. "Well, you guys are pretty cute, too," he said. And after that, Plum and Keeker figured the groundhogs would probably be okay. Phew!

"Hmmmm," said Mr. Dana. Keeker just *knew*
he was thinking about groundhog holes.

"Don't worry, Dad," said Keeker. "I know
what to do. Let's move the whole groundhog
family to the field behind the barn. It's not used
for horses anymore, so they can dig all the
holes they want!"

Mr. Dana thought it was a great idea. He
asked Keeker to lead Plum into the field, so the
groundhogs would follow.

The field behind the barn was overgrown,
with lots of long grass and all kinds of wild-
flowers—daisies, clover, cornflowers, and even
black-eyed Susans.

Mrs. Groundhog loved it right away. So did
her pups—as soon as they were inside the gate,
they went squeaking off in different directions
to explore their new home.

Plum was *very* relieved. So was Keeker.

The whole rest of the day, Keeker and her parents stayed in the barn, watching Rosie and giving Pansy lots of treats and kisses. Plum hung around, too, in case anyone wanted to give *her* any treats. "After all," thought Plum, "Pansy isn't the only one who's had a busy day!"

For dinner, Keeker's mom put together a picnic basket and brought it down to the barn. Pretty soon it was bedtime—but no one felt like going back to the house.

"We could just camp out down here tonight,"
suggested Keeker's dad. "And Plum could stay in
her stall instead of going back down to the field."

"Well," thought Plum. "I suppose I could hang
around for a bit . . ."

Keeker and her mom and dad put hay bales
together to make two big beds. Then they
piled a ton of blankets and sleeping bags on top.
Camping in the barn was so fun!

Plum decided to sleep standing up so she could keep an eye on Rosie. (Rosie was kind of cute, after all.)

Rosie curled up next to her delicious warm-smelling mother. And in the field behind the barn, the groundhogs dug a comfy hole and pig-piled on top of each other.

All over Vermont, mamas and babies were snuggled up tight. The flowers in the field closed up their petals. And the big quiet earth rocked them all to sleep.

GALLOPING YOUR WAY IN FALL 2007

Introducing a new adventure in the Sneaky Pony series

KEEKER

and the Pony Camp Catastrophe

Keeker and Plum are SO excited! They get to go to sleepaway camp for girls and their ponies for a whole week. When they arrive, Keeker is pleased to discover that Camp Kickapoo looks just as she expected. Fun soon turns to frustration when Keeker's group gets stuck learning riding techniques that Keeker thinks are way too babyish. But when another camper's spirited pony bolts, Keeker and her friends prove that they can handle difficult riding challenges.